YO Mike!
Johnny and I wish
you the best at MI.
Be sure to impress
them with your dance
moves. CHET ☆

Michael,
    Your Ogre's Slump is one of the best
I have ever seen. Keep up the good work.

                                -Professor Knight

Hey Killer —
I hear you're off to Monsters Inc.
Don't get caught in a mail chute.

                                J Worthington

Remember when we tried out for <u>A Midsummer Night's Scream</u>? You were ˗AMAZING!!!˗ Oh, wait. Wrong Mike. Have a great summer, anyway

—Wesley Rao

I KNOW YOU'RE GOING TO GO FAR, BUDDY.

JUST REMEMBER THE LATE, GREAT ARTHUR CLAWSON'S WORDS:

"KNOWLEDGE MUST NEVER BE FEARED,

WISDOM MUST ALWAYS BE PURSUED,

AND EXCELLENCE MUST BE AT THE CENTER OF EVERYTHING."

GOOD LUCK AT MI!

—BARRY McMAHON

 BOO!

Mikey,

I just loved having you in the house this year. I'll miss the pitter-patter of your little green feet coming to the kitchen for my bluescary pie! You come back and visit anytime!

Sheri Squibbles

Disney · PIXAR

MONSTERS UNIVERSITY

~~YEARBOOK~~ FEAR

1313

Mike!
I didn't get to know You
very well this Year but
You seem like a cool guy.

Keep Smiling!
RAY!

Mike,
Your smile is winning!
Keep in touch, ok? :
Tay ♥

MONSTERS
— UNIVERSITY —
VALID FALL/SPRING SEMESTER
M. Wazowski
STUDENT
Scaring
MAJOR
Mike Wazowski
SIGNATURE   ID NO. 600962011054255

CONTENTS

Mike,

It was really nice getting to know you and hanging out at ~~my mom's~~ the OK fraternity house. I had a great time building pillow forts together.

Your pal,

Scott Squibbles

6 CAMPUS LIFE

11 ACADEMICS

22 GOING GREEK

33 STUDENT CLUBS

37 SPORTS

43 FACULTY AND STUDENTS

MONSTERS
—UNIVERSITY—

Founded in 1313 by Arthur Clawson, Monsters University has been a leading center of scholarship, scientific innovation, and juvenile hijinks since it first opened its towering gates.

This yearbook documents a single year of student life at Monsters University, but there are centuries of history behind it. As you revisit the year that was, we hope you are reminded of the many years that came before.

Arthur Clawson, 1313.

The Monsters University of today: where modernity meets history, and some truly scary stuff happens.

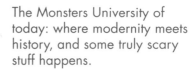

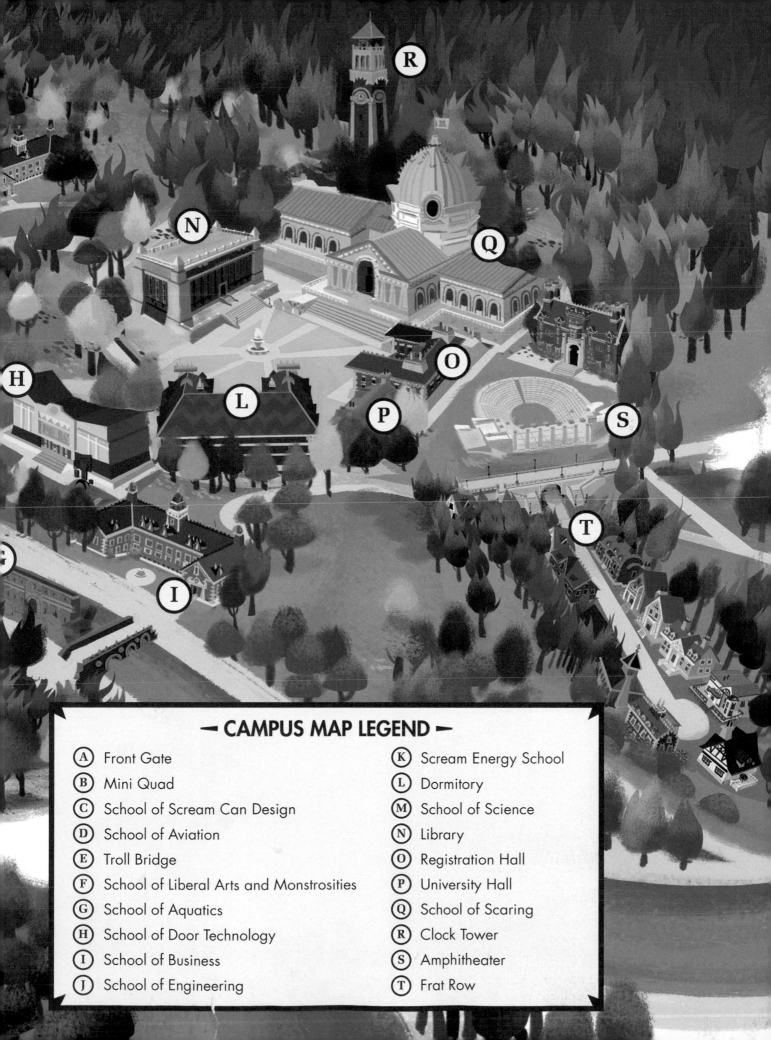

— CAMPUS MAP LEGEND —

- (A) Front Gate
- (B) Mini Quad
- (C) School of Scream Can Design
- (D) School of Aviation
- (E) Troll Bridge
- (F) School of Liberal Arts and Monstrosities
- (G) School of Aquatics
- (H) School of Door Technology
- (I) School of Business
- (J) School of Engineering
- (K) Scream Energy School
- (L) Dormitory
- (M) School of Science
- (N) Library
- (O) Registration Hall
- (P) University Hall
- (Q) School of Scaring
- (R) Clock Tower
- (S) Amphitheater
- (T) Frat Row

CAMPUS LIFE

MU students were a busy bunch this year. When they weren't in class, or at sports practice, or attending club meetings, they could be found hanging out all over campus, studying, talking, and even napping! Dorm lobbies were a popular place for students to gather, as was the quad.

After the cafeteria closed up for the night, students often headed to The Growl for a snack and some conversation. Known far and wide for its famous chili cheese flies, The Growl is practically a campus institution.

FRESHMEN START THE YEAR WITH A SMILE!

There are few things more exciting in a monster's life than the first day of college, and this year was no exception.

"I have been working my entire life for this moment!" said freshman Mike Wazowski. "I'm going to be a Scarer!"

A Scare School student hits the books!

On hand to greet and guide the new students was the Smile Squad—and the group's name sure was accurate. Whether directing students to their new dorm rooms or showing them the activities fair, this happy crew never stopped grinning.

Smile Squad members Ray, Trey, Fay, Jay, and Kay greet the incoming freshmen with—you guessed it—smiles!

SCHOOL SPIRIT IS KING AT MONSTERS UNIVERSITY

Monsters University isn't the kind of school you end up at by accident. Ask any student here, and they're likely to tell you they've been dreaming of attending MU since they were a larva, grub, egg, puggle, or chick.

"Dude, I was born for this school," one monster told us as he displayed his blue and white body. He was just one example of the fierce loyalty MU students showed their school. Many students wore clothing with the MU logo on it, especially the popular four-sleeved hoodie, and the campus bookstore sold a wide variety of MU-branded objects such as fangbrushes, horn wax, juice glasses, sleeping bags, wing cozies, knitting needles, hubcaps, and odorant. Rumor has it they also sell books, though this has not been substantiated.

MU RULES!

HOMECOMING

A Day of Fun in the Sun for Every Monster!

Two MU alumni share a secret handshake.

When the leaves start changing color and the air gets crisp, students at MU know it's almost time for homecoming. Every year, more than a thousand MU students and alumni attend Homecoming Weekend, and the most popular event—after the football game, of course—is always the parade.

And what a parade it was!

"I've never seen anything like it!" gushed freshman Randy Boggs. "The floats! The marching band! The Homecoming Queen!" Boggs said before disappearing entirely. "She's beautiful," he continued. Or someone did. (As Mr. Boggs was no longer visible, this quote cannot be attributed to him with any certainty.)

All in all, it was a glorious Homecoming Weekend!

Homecoming Queen Stephanie Dallmar presided over the parade with glamour and grace.

STUDENT CLUBS DRAW BIG SPEAKERS

While many student groups invited guest speakers onto campus this year, the most impressive by far was clearly Monsters University Scare Program graduate Frightening Frank McKay.

"Cherish these years, kids," McKay told students. "You've got everything you need here at Monsters University. Good friends, lots of parties, a roof over your heads . . . why, it feels like you've got all the slime in the world. Your professors at Monsters University are getting you ready for real life. It's a cold, hard world out there, kids. You gotta be faster, meaner, and hairier than the next guy. It's eat or be eaten. You gotta look out for number one. It's all about survival of the fittest. Anything that doesn't kill you makes you stronger.

"Also, you should probably learn to do your own laundry."

ACADEMICS

From the natural sciences to the liberal arts, Monsters University students took advantage of a wide variety of courses this year. Brothers Terri and Terry Perry especially enjoyed their world literature course. "It's a lot of reading," Terri said. "But with two heads, even a fourteen-hundred-page book goes pretty fast."

"We trade chapters," Terry explained. "It can get pretty confusing, but it's very efficient."

Monsters U students may have partied hard this year, but they studied even harder.

SCHOOL OF SCARING

The Fine Art of Horror

The most prestigious and competitive program at Monsters University is, without doubt, the Scare School. If this program sometimes seems cruelly competitive, it's for a good reason. Students who graduate with a Scaring degree will be true masters of the topic. An MU Scare graduate can tell you what philosophers have written about the nature of fear itself . . . and also what the best way is to scare the pants off an eight-year-old from Kenya who's afraid of dinosaurs and ladybugs.

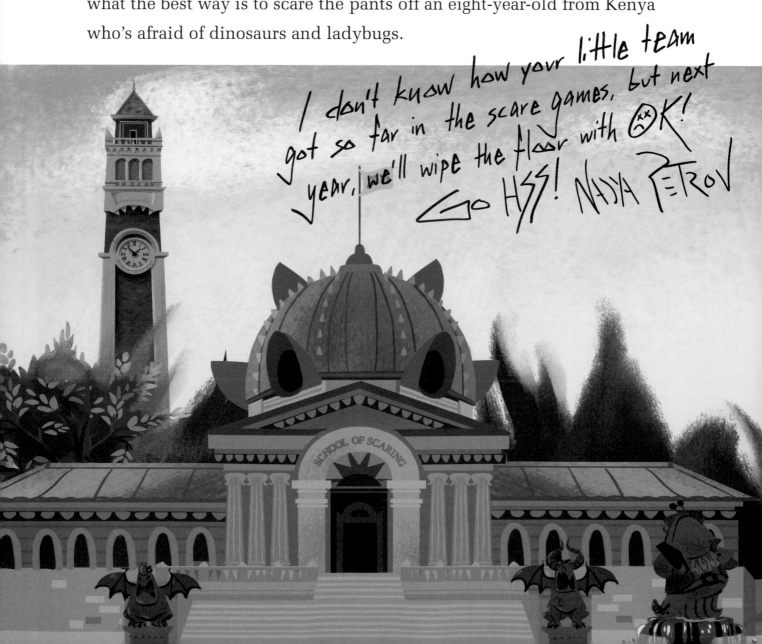

I don't know how your little team got so far in the scare games, but next year, we'll wipe the floor with OK! Go HSS! NADYA PETROV

 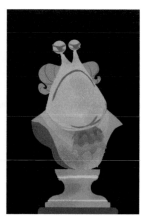  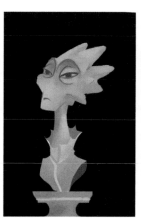 

Notable alumni and faculty are honored in the halls of the Scare School.

Mike, I'll never forget the look
on Hardscrabble's face when
that scream canister broke.
Classic!! Good luck
next year!!!
Tommy Flaggerton

At the head of this famous school is Dean Hardscrabble. A legendary Scarer herself, Abigail Hardscrabble broke the all-time scare record with a scream that, until recently, resided in the scare can displayed beneath her portrait. In a great scandal for the Scare School, the can was destroyed this year as the result of grossly inappropriate and irresponsible behavior by two students.

Dean Hardscrabble, as inspiring as she is terrifying!

SCHOOL OF ENGINEERING

Leading the (Door) Way

A Portal Connectivity senior tests his final project for the first time. Congratulations! It's a working door!

Door Technicians provide a fundamental building block of modern monster society. There would be no scaring without doors, and therefore no scare power.

This year's Door Tech students worked hard learning to design and make doors leading to the human world. While most of their time was spent mastering the complex engineering principles behind door manufacturing, some Door Tech majors admit their favorite class was carpentry.

The Fascinating Science of . . . Cans.

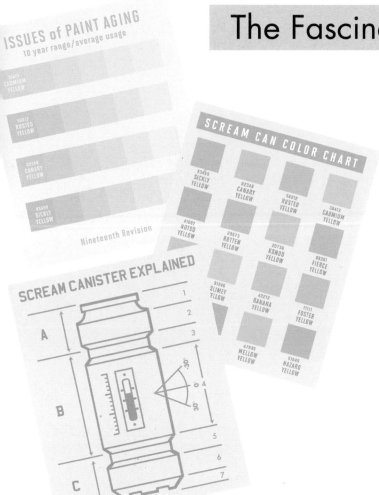

ISSUES of PAINT AGING
10 year range/average usage

CADMIUM
YELLOW

RUSTED
YELLOW

CANARY
YELLOW

SICKLY
YELLOW

Nineteenth Revision

SCREAM CAN COLOR CHART

SICKLY
YELLOW

CANARY
YELLOW

RUSTED
YELLOW

CADMIUM
YELLOW

NOTSO
YELLOW

ROTTEN
YELLOW

KONDO
YELLOW

FIERCE
YELLOW

SLIMEY
YELLOW

BANANA
YELLOW

FOSTER
YELLOW

MELLOW
YELLOW

HAZARD
YELLOW

SCREAM CANISTER EXPLAINED

A

B

C

1
2
3
4
5
6
7

Scream Can Design may not be the most exciting or glamorous line of study at MU, but scream can designers are a part of the scare-industrial complex. Without these dogged can-design engineers toiling thanklessly over the frankly very boring question of how to best cram screams into metal tubes . . . honestly, things would probably still be pretty much the same.

On the plus side, Can Designers are the only ones who know every shade of yellow that scare cans come in!

Professor Brandywine teaches students the art of Scream Canister construction.

SCHOOL OF LIBERAL ARTS AND MONSTROSITIES

Students Get in Touch with Their Softer Sides

Monsters Lit students discuss the classics.

MU students have always excelled in the scare-related fields, but that's not all we're about. Many students graduated this year with degrees in literature, music, fine art, and even philosophy.

VINCENT LEE

The Monstrosities department has always believed that a well-rounded education makes for well-rounded monsters. So whether it was a lively lit-class discussion of *Slime and Punishment* or a field trip to see a production of *My Scare Lady*, Monsters University strove to open students' minds and broaden their horizons. After all, a big part of what makes a Scarer great is a good sense of theatrics!

KEEP ON LIVIN', LAUGHIN', & CRYIN'. AND KEEP UP the DREAM JOURNAL, MAN. ∴ HUGS, ART

Yoga students learn about spiritualism and philosophy as they flex.

SCHOOL OF BUSINESS

$$\frac{-\hbar^2}{2m} \nabla^2 \Psi(r) + V(r)\Psi(r)$$

$$= \text{Fun for Everyone!}$$

Professor Crabacus is a star of the Accounting department.

$$\frac{ROAR}{GROWL} \quad R = GWSY \quad R = \sqrt{\frac{ws}{y}}$$
$$R^2 = \sqrt{R^2 O a^2 R} \quad G = \sqrt{\frac{ys}{w}}$$
$$Lp\,(dBSPL) = 20 \cdot \log(10)^P \quad p\,\frac{Lp\,(dBSPL)}{20}$$
$$P_0 = 0.00002\,Pa \quad p(Pa) = \frac{P_0}{P_0\,10}$$

Business classes at Monsters University aren't just for eggheads and pencil-necked geeks with pocket protectors—they're also for snaggle-fangs, cyclopes, and anyone else who's interested.

From the always-popular City Destroying class to the graduate-level Fuzzy Math seminar taught by the legendary Professor Crabacus (and only open to students with a 4.0 GPA and fur longer than three inches), MU offered students a wide variety of classes to stimulate the left side of their brains.

The departments of City Planning and City Destroying hard at work.

Paul Wooten

A Computer Science major shows us how it's done!

SCHOOL OF SCIENCE

Junior Vishal Gupta exits the Aviation building.

This year Monsters University offered a wide range of aquatic courses, with more students than ever taking advantage of the extensive underwater rivers that flow through the foundations of this ancient campus. Similarly, aviation classes such as Flying for Winged Monsters and Advanced Flight Maneuvers were held high in the towers of the Aviation building, reachable only by winged students and faculty.

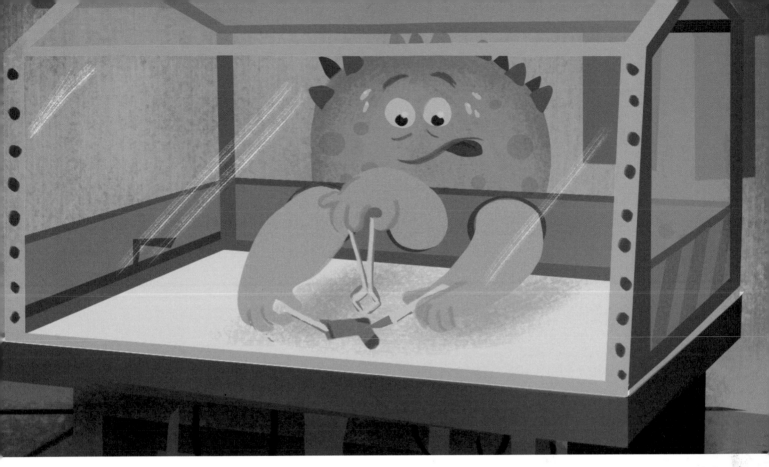

Students studying Advanced Sock Dissection handled real children's socks. The strictest levels of quarantine were always observed.

But it wasn't just air- and water-based monsters who had a wealth of classes to choose from. Students from a variety of disciplines were able to find classes to meet their interests, including Ocular Study and Advanced Plant Study.

No matter how obscure the topic, there was probably someone teaching it at MU.

Students worked with state-of-the-art lab equipment in Introduction to Slimeology.

Nature lovers always enjoy botany classes!

GOING GR**Σ**Σ**K**

A beloved tradition at Monsters University, fraternities and sororities have always been a place for students to make friends, rise to new challenges, and learn good old-fashioned monster values. This year's new EEK pledges learned the importance of constant scare training, while JOX taught its members the importance of constant partying.

Sororities and fraternities are a vital part of the rich student life here at MU, and as the annual Scare Games proved, the houses continue to get better every year.

Mike,
I've always admired your endless enthusiasm.
GO MU,
Claire Wheeler

THE GREEK COUNCIL

You Can't Spell "Greek" Without "Eek"!

Claire Wheeler and Brock Pearson were unlikely partners, but they got the job done!

The Greek Council oversees all aspects of fraternity and sorority life here at Monsters University. This year it outdid itself, organizing a weeklong community service effort that resulted in a forty-foot-deep sinkhole just off campus. "It swallowed eight cars and an I-Scream, You-Scream frozen treats truck," said Greek Council vice president Brock Pearson. "That was one hungry sinkhole!"

Claire Wheeler and Brock Pearson, the current heads of the Greek Council, not only led this governing body, but were also personally responsible for the yearly Scare Games—arguably the most important event on campus, and certainly the biggest job for the Greek Council.

With all eyes (and antennae) on campus trained on the council and its leadership, the pressure was enormous. But Claire and Brock proved they were worthy of the task. They put together the most grueling, humiliating, and downright intimidating course yet for the Scare Games. And they did it with skill, grace, and, of course, ruthless brutality!

RΩR

ROAR OMEGA ROAR

Front: Reggie Jacobs, Chet Alexander
Back: Chip Goff, Randy Boggs, Johnny Worthington, Javier Rios

One of the oldest fraternities at Monsters University, ROR is simply the best of the best. The ROR brothers, led by president Johnny Worthington, live to win. Nothing is more important to them than scaring, and it shows. ROR brothers truly are the blue bloods of the MU campus.

PNK

PYTHON NU KAPPA

They may be as vain as Venus flytraps, but everyone knows the PNKs are also fierce competitors in the Scare Games. And no one is scarier than their president, Carrie Williams, who once turned down a modeling job because she only wanted to be a spokesperson for a crematorium or a taxidermist. These gorgeous sorority sisters take scaring very seriously and are major contenders at the Scare Games every year. There is one chink in their cheery, perky, glossy armor, though: chick flicks. Their current favorite is *All About Evil*.

From left to right: Crystal Du Bois, Carrie Williams, Heather Olson, Britney Davis, Taylor Holbrook, Naomi Jackson

hey Mike, I'll trade my big wings for your big brains!

JOX

Fly high! Chaz Harris

JAWS THETA CHI

Nobody would accuse the brothers of Jaws Theta Chi of being the brainiest guys on campus. But people would—and do!—accuse them of cheating, roughhousing, and intimidation tactics. These muscle-bound brothers took their cues this year from president Roy "Big Red" O'Growlahan, who started every morning with a five-gallon protein shake. The JOX are obsessed with scaring. Once they get going, nothing can stop them.

From left to right: Percy Boleslaw, Dirk Pratt, Roy O'Growlahan, George Sanderson, Omar Harris, Baboso Gortega

HSS

ETA HISS HISS

NO ORDER

Front: Nancy Kim, Sonia Lewis
Back: Susan Jensen, Rosie Levin, Nadya Petrov, Rhonda Boyd

Sullen, angry, and decked out in all black, the sisters of HSS are even more intense than their perky counterparts at PNK. President Rosie Levin is trained in Chewjitsu and is rumored to get a new earring every time she makes a grown monster cry. HSS began as a secret society the year Monsters University was founded. Nobody who is not a HSS has seen the inside of their sorority house and lived to tell the tale.

When they aren't scaring, the ladies of HSS perform together as an award-winning a cappella group!

ΣΣΚ

Carla Delgado

SLUGMA SLUGMA KAPPA

From left to right: Maria Garcia, Debbie Gabler, Donna Soohoo, Brynn Larson, Violet Steslicki, Carla Delgado

UN STOP ABLE

UNDERWATER SCARE OFF

With notable alumnae such as Carla "Killer Claws" Benitez, the EEKs have a reputation for being serious contenders in the Scare Games, and they work hard to keep it that way. These athletic sorority sisters never leave the house without sweatbands, just in case there's time for a quick workout in between classes or during a date.

OK

OOZMA KAPPA

One of MU's newer fraternities, OK has become a haven for aspiring Scarers who have been cut from the Scare Program. These scrappy newcomers took the university by storm this year with their terrific performance at the Scare Games. OK certainly has heart to spare—and now we know they've got Scare to spare, too.

A wild Saturday night at OK!

Front row: Scott Squibbles, Don Carlton, Michael Wazowski
Back row: Art, James Sullivan, Terri Perry, Terry Perry

LITTLE MAN ON CAMPUS! THAT WAS QUITE AN "OK" PERFORMANCE YOU GAVE AT THIS YEAR'S SCARE GAMES! OOOOOOZMAAA!!

BROCK PEARSON

THE SCARE GAMES

SCARE GAMES

FINAL SIGN UP JAN. 25

PROVE YOU'RE THE BEST

The Scare Games, founded by our very own Dean Hardscrabble, are a big part of Greek life. But this year they weren't just a big deal—they were *the* big deal. Of the six Greek houses that enrolled in the games, five were frequent competitors: ROR, EEK, JOX, PNK, and HSS have all been in the games for at least the last ten years. But in a surprise twist, an upstart house came out of nowhere and entered the games as well: Oozma Kappa, a.k.a. OK, performing better than expected.

Things got tense as house after house was eliminated. By the fifth round, it was down to OK and ROR.

At first, OK performed terribly, which, frankly, was what everyone expected. But as the events went on, OK began showing real skill—and real teamwork.

OK's success was a shocking turn: it had gone from being an obscure team to being a real threat to the unmovable champions, ROR. It was a Scare Games to remember.

ROR has captured the coveted Scare Games trophy for the last three years running.

George Sanderson

Top: The members of Jaws Theta Chi complete the Toxicity Challenge.

Midde: OK frat member Mike Wazowski evades detection during the Hiding event.

SCARE GAME HIGHLIGHTS

Bottom: There's nothing scarier than a HSS girl! If that wooden child could Scream, you'd hear him for miles!

IMPROV CLUB

FILM SOCIETY

BOOK WORMS

GLEE

green team

STUDENT CLUBS—

CRAWLING WITH CREATIVITY!

Whether they were acting, singing, or arranging poisonous flowers, Monsters University students found ways to enrich their lives with the many clubs hosted on campus! New-Age Philosophy major Art's favorite club this year was Yogis United for Knowledge, or YUK. "Yoga isn't just about bending yourself into a grotesque, quivering, sweating pretzel," Art said. "It's also really deep. You learn stuff about yourself. I'm still trying to master Child's Pose, and it's like looking into the heart of darkness, man."

With all the student clubs on campus, it's a wonder MU students got any classwork done at all!

GLEE CLUB

This year, there was music everywhere on campus. From the bathrooms in the School of Engineering to the snake-infested caverns of the maintenance tunnels, Monsters University's barbershop quartet always had a song to share—whether you wanted to hear it or not!

Have an ooey, gooey summer!
ROARS & whispers,
Elektra Demapoulos

ART CLUB

Monsters University students might be the scariest around, but they're also sensitive and artistic. With workshops for watercolor painting, needlepoint, pottery, and interpretive belching, the Art Club gave students a place to express their inner selves in an accepting—and well-armored—environment.

Turner Dowrton

BOOKWORMS

Subsisting on a nourishing diet of classic literature, romance, mysteries, and science fiction, the Bookworms just couldn't get enough this year! They ravenously devoured more than a hundred books, meeting regularly to discuss their favorites. "We're voracious, uh, readers," said one Bookworm. "I have no idea why we've been banned from the library."

EMMETT FRANCO

DEBATE TEAM

The spirit of discourse is a strong tradition at Monsters University. But no one works as hard at trivial nitpicking as the debate team. This year, the Monsters University Debate Team dominated the collegiate debate division, taking home three regional cups and placing in the Monster Melee semifinals before being disqualified for taking both sides at once.

YEARBOOK

Here at the Monsters University Yearbook, our top priority is to bring you a book bulging with hard-hitting journalism, action-packed photography, and cherished memories.

This year's especially candid photography was handled by Lane Picca, who gives new meaning to the word "intrepid." And to the word "intrusive," and also the word "insane." She'll do anything for the perfect shot! Thanks for your great work, Lane. Good luck with all those restraining orders.

Lane Picca

THE CAMPUS ROAR

It was an eventful year at Monsters University, and *The Campus Roar* was there to report on every story. From the dizzying heights of the Aviation School to the murky depths of the bottomless swimming pool, the newspaper's dedicated reporters got the stories out.

SPORTS

Collegiate life at Monsters University isn't just about hitting the books. This year, the Athletics department made sure of that, with even the most obscure sports thriving.

"This was our best year yet!" said Jod Jone, president of the Monsters University Potato Sack Racing Society. "We finally have two members—so we can actually have a race!"

From trying out for the football team to volunteering first-aid services to the victims of chess matches, MU students found countless sports to get their blood—and bile—pumping.

PNK rules! We'll get OK next year ♥ Taylor

FOOTBALL

MU Tramples the Competition!

The sun was high in the sky, not a cloud to be seen. A foul breeze wafted over the field. The crowd held its collective sulfurous breath. The score was 25–27, with Fear Tech in the lead. The clock was running out. With seconds to spare, MU halfback Van Earl, Jr., made a glorious sprint, his gelatinous form bouncing and quivering as he raced his way across the field at top speed. But the speed was too much for Earl's goo-based body, and his top half separated from his bottom half during the final stretch of his run. After a brief conference, the referees decided a touchdown executed by only half a player was still a valid play.

MU Football Season Totals:

Rushing Yards: 6,171
Rushing Yards per Game: 440.8
Slithering Yards: 4,882
Slithering Yards per Game: 384.7
Points: 470
Points per Game: 33.6
Pointy Things: 11
Pointy Things per Game: 0.78 (an all-time low)

Score! Monsters University won the big game against archrival Fear Tech!

This year was just one in a long and storied history of football here at Monsters University. And thanks to the breathless excitement of games like MU vs. Fear Tech, the stands at MU were packed all season long.

Stats

Game Highlights:

Vs. **Fear Tech**:
MU 22 FT 27

Of note: Two TDs were scored by Fear Tech quarterback Jeff "Digger" McGee, who tunneled beneath the field into the end zone.

Vs. **Creature College**:
MU 35 CC 18

Of note: One of the pep squad's pom-poms went missing during the game. It was later discovered in the equipment room cozying up to a spare football.

Vs. **Viscous State**:
MU 26 VS 25

Of note: Both teams were momentarily blinded when a panicked VS linebacker released noxious gas into the air as a defense mechanism.

ZP1117 211 G 17
1 GENADM 1 1 EZP1117
398 1
Z2 75Y 398
$ 12.00 MONSTERS UNIVERSITY Z2 75Y
J 21 VS. $ 12.00
ZWS0915 FEAR TECH J 21
FRI OCT 16 8:00PM ZWS0915

TICKET

BEST OF RIVALS

Freshman James Sullivan celebrates capturing Archie the Scare Pig.

For as long as Monsters University and Fear Tech have existed, these two prestigious schools have been bitter rivals. This year saw a major triumph for Monsters University with the abduction of Fear Tech's mascot, Archie the Scare Pig, by freshman James Sullivan.

Fear Tech and Monsters University take their rivalry seriously, but it's all in good fun. Why, nobody's been maimed or even seriously hurt . . . *this* year!

BEAT FEAR TECH!

Marching to Her Own Beat!

MARCHING BAND

The MU Marching Band had a great year, combining expert musicianship with the demanding athleticism of, well, walking around. Whether rehearsing MU fight songs or mapping out new marching patterns, this dedicated monster trained constantly.

PEP SQUAD

Rah! Rah! Hiss Boom Bah!

No sporting event at Monsters University would be complete without the eardrum-piercing cries of the Pep Squad.

The entire squad was present at every sporting event of the season, even some that took place simultaneously. The Pep Squad has not offered an explanation for this, and nobody has dared ask for one.

PING-PONG TEAM

The King Kong of Ping-Pong Shows Us How It's Done!

The Monsters University table tennis team had a record-breaking year, which was also its first year, thanks to its founding (and only) member, Zane Xiao. Xiao, a freshman, has had a passion for the sport since his grandmonster taught him to play when he was a grub. Employing the controversial "tripaddle" technique, Xiao was able to face up to three opponents at once.

CREW TEAM Paddling for Victory!

For students living near the river, the sound of the coxswain yelling "Stroke! Stroke!" at five in the morning was a frequent (and unwelcome) wake-up call. The MU crew team, best known for the powerful lungs of its coxswain, Buster "Birdy" McBride, was joined this year by rising star Russell Woodruff. Unfortunately, the team performed abysmally overall. Many blame the extraordinary size of the other team members: the smallest of them weighed in at 525 pounds!

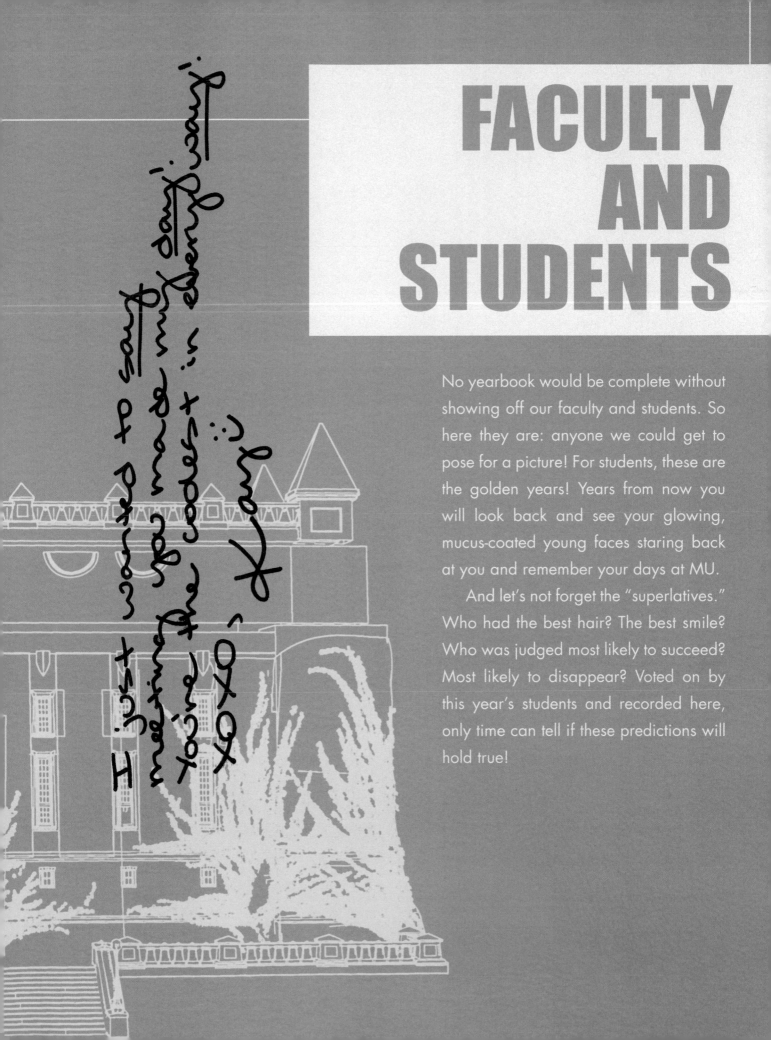

FACULTY AND STUDENTS

No yearbook would be complete without showing off our faculty and students. So here they are: anyone we could get to pose for a picture! For students, these are the golden years! Years from now you will look back and see your glowing, mucus-coated young faces staring back at you and remember your days at MU.

And let's not forget the "superlatives." Who had the best hair? The best smile? Who was judged most likely to succeed? Most likely to disappear? Voted on by this year's students and recorded here, only time can tell if these predictions will hold true!

I just wanted to say
meetings you made my day!
to join the coolest in eternity.
XOXO, Karl :)
love you always.

FACULTY

SCREAM CAN DESIGN
William Brandywine

MATHEMATICS
Brian Corbis

DEAN OF SCARING
Abigail Hardscrabble

SLIMEOLOGY
Jerome Humbert

DRAMA
Henrietta Foster

LIBRARIAN
Margaret Gesner

MONSTRIOLOGY
Bonholm Klinker

SCARING
Derek Knight

FACULTY

BUSINESS LOGISTICS
Carlton N. Masse

LITERATURE
Harriett Munn

ACCOUNTING
Timothy Rastrussen

POTTERY
Vasantha Sitron

DEAN OF ATHLETICS
Elmer Niven

SCREAM ENERGY
Rufus Oozeman

NEW AGE PHILOSOPHY
Filbert Turbeek

AVIATION
Cathy Wilsterbury

STUDENTS

Chet Alexander
Hakim Al-Saidi
Art
Kwesi Balewa
Jennifer Bantle
Anthony Battle
Michelle Bauer

Joseph Beissel
Kenneth Bird
Flora Blob-Ghast
Sylvester Blorp
Randy Boggs
Percy Boleslaw
Christophe Booker

Rhonda Boyd
Donald Burch
David Cahill
Oswald Calloway
Don Carlton
Eric Carney
Claire Carver

Keith Castaneda
Cynthia Chan
Tae-Kun Cho
Larry Cohen
Jerry Cote
Hap Coulter
Stephanie Dallmar

Cynthia Chan

STUDENTS

Wayne Dautch

Britney Davis

Jay de Cay

Carla Delgado

Elektra Demopoulos

Sandra Dillard

Turner Dourton

Philip Drewel

Crystal Du Bois

Robert Duke

Bertram Fitzmonster

Tommy Flaggerton

Craig Foreman

Emmett Franco

Solivia Froth

Harry Furn

Debbie Gabler

Maria Garcia

Rodney Garcia

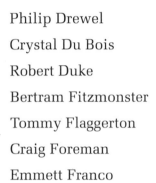

Julie
Gillespie ⟶

Eliza Gash

Olga Gasparov

John Geiger

Julie Gillespie

Siegel Gnash

BEST HAIR
Michelle Bauer

STUDENTS

Chip Goff
Baboso Gortega
Gary Goyle
Vishal Gupta
Douglas Hall
Omar Harris
Lisa Heck

Carl Hinton
Taylor Holbrook
Bryan Holcomb
Dawn Hooper
Brian Hubert
Jason Hubert
Jeremy Hubert

Michael Hubert
Naomi Jackson
Reggie Jacobs
Hornetta James
Susan Jensen

Jod Jone
Nancy Kim
Todd Kirkland
Melissa Knapp
Binh Lam

MOST STUDIOUS
Mike Wazowski

~wishing you a summer full of gross, gruesome things! 🖤 Naomi♡

 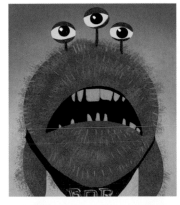  

STUDENTS

Brynn Larson
Vincent Lee
Rosie Levin
Bradley Levy
Sonia Lewis
Phyllis Longslime
Glen Lopez

Curtis Martinez
Mark McDermott
Snuk McGert
Barry McMahon
Stingrid Michaelson
Walter Mooney
Hämeenlinna Myllylä

Brad Nosferatski
Kay O'Day
Roy O'Growlahan

Ryan O'Horn
Heather Olson
Carol Owens

MOST LIKELY TO DISAPPEAR
Randy Boggs

STUDENTS

Willie Park

Burton Payne

Brock Pearson

Terri Perry

Terry Perry

Nadya Petrov

Jose Petty

Lane Picca

Dirk Pratt

Jane Pratt

Wesley Rao

Harold Raritan

Stephen Rasmussen

Darren Ratliff

Daniel Riggs

Javier Rios

Kayleigh Robinson

Ronald Rocha

Tammy Rollins

Wanda Rosales

Gregory Sampson

George Sanderson

Emma Scratchet

Trey Shea

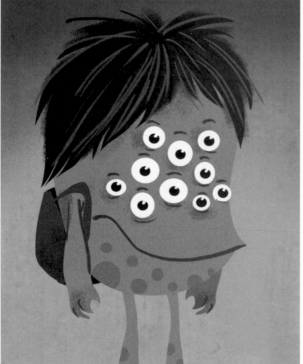

MOST VISIONARY
Mark McDermott

STUDENTS

Victor Singh
Robert Skaren
Lydia Skink
Darryl Snagglebottom
Robert Sobotka
Donna Soohoo
Albert Sosa

Scott Squibbles
Violet Steslicki
Maggie Stillwater
Manami Sugiyama
James Sullivan
Ralph Terrell
Weiqin Tsui

Ray Veigh
Furgie von Limbergoop
Pamela Walker
Mike Wazowski
Fay Wei

Claire Wheeler
Carrie Williams
Paul Wooten
Johnny Worthington
Adolfo Zaragoza

MOST LIKELY TO SUCCEED
James Sullivan

MEMORIES

Alexander, Chet 24, 48
Al-Saidi, Hakim 48
Archie the Scare Pig 40
Art 17, 29, 33, 48, 60
Art Club 34
Balewa, Kwesi 49
Bantle, Jennifer 49
Battle, Anthony 49
Bauer, Michelle 49, 51
Beissel, Joseph 48
Bird, Kenneth 48
Blob-Ghast, Flora 48
Blorp, Sylvester 49
Boggs, Randy 9, 24, 49, 54, 61
Boleslaw, Percy 26, 32, 49
Booker, Christophe 49
Bookworms 35
Boyd, Rhonda 27, 48
Brandywine, William 15, 44
Burch, Donald 48
Cahill, David 48
Calloway, Oswald 49
Campus Roar, The 36
Carlton, Don 19, 29, 49, 60
Carney, Eric 49
Carver, Claire 49
Castaneda, Keith 36, 48
Chan, Cynthia 48
Cho, Tae-Kun 48
City Destroying 18, 19
City Planning 18, 19
Clawson, Arthur 3
Cohen, Larry 49
Corbis, Brian 44
Cote, Jerry 49
Coulter, Hap 49
Crabacus, Professor 18
Creature College 39
Crew Team 42
Dallmar, Stephanie 9, 49
Dautch, Wayne 50
Davis, Britney 25, 50
de Cay, Jay 7, 50
Debate Team 35
Delgado, Carla 28, 51
Demopoulos, Elektra 34, 51
Dillard, Sandra 51
Door Technology 14
Dourton, Turner 34, 51
Drewel, Philip 50
Du Bois, Crystal 25, 50
Duke, Robert 50
Earl, Van, Jr. 38

EEK 22, 28, 30
Fear Tech 38, 39, 40
Fitzmonster, Bertram 51
Flaggerton, Tommy 36, 51
Football 38-39
Foreman, Craig 51
Foster, Henrietta 45
Franco, Emmett 35, 51
Froth, Solivia 3, 50
Furn, Harry 50
Gabler, Debbie 28, 50
Garcia, Maria 28, 51
Garcia, Rodney 51
Gash, Eliza 50
Gasparov, Olga 50
Geiger, John 50
Gesner, Margaret 45
Gillespie, Julie 51
Glee Club 34
Gnash, Siegel 51
Goff, Chip 24, 52
Gortega, Baboso 26, 32, 52
Goyle, Gary 52
Greek Council 23
Gupta, Vishal 20, 53
Hall, Douglas 53
Hardscrabble, Abigail 13, 30, 44
Harris, Omar 26, 32, 53
Heck, Lisa 36, 53
Hinton, Carl 52
Holbrook, Taylor 25, 52
Holcomb, Bryan 36, 52
homecoming 9
Hooper, Dawn 53
HSS 27, 30, 32
Hubert, Brian 34, 53
Hubert, Jason 34, 53
Hubert, Jeremy 34, 53
Hubert, Michael 34, 52
Humbert, Jerome 44
Jackson, Naomi 25, 53
Jacobs, Reggie 24, 53
James, Hornetta 53
Jensen, Susan 27, 53
Jone, Jod 37, 52
JOX 22, 26, 30, 32
Kim, Nancy 27, 53
Kirkland, Todd 53
Klinker, Bonholm 45
Knapp, Melissa 53
Knight, Derek 45
Lam, Binh 53
Larson, Brynn 28, 54

Lee, Vincent 17, 54
Levin, Rosie 27, 54
Levy, Bradley 55
Lewis, Sonia 27, 55
Longslime, Phyllis 35, 55
Lopez, Glen 55
Marching Band 41
Martinez, Curtis 36, 54
Masse, Carlton 46
McBride, Buster "Birdy" 42
McDermott, Mark 54, 56
McGee, Jeff "Digger" 39
McGert, Snuk 54
McKay, Frightening Frank 10
McMahon, Barry 55
Michaelson, Stingrid 55
Mooney, Walter 55
Munn, Harriett 16, 46
Myllylä, Hämeelinna 55
Niven, Elmer 47
Nosferatski, Brad 35, 54
O'Day, Kay 7, 55
O'Growlahan, Roy 26, 32, 55
O'Horn, Ryan 36, 54
OK 29, 30, 31, 32
Olson, Heather 25, 55
Oozeman, Rufus 47
Owens, Carol 55
Park, Willie 56
Payne, Burton 56
Pearson, Brock 23, 31, 56, 60
Pep Squad 41
Perry, Terri 11, 29, 57, 60
Perry, Terry 11, 29, 57, 60
Petrov, Nadya 27, 32, 57
Petty, Jose 57
Picca, Lane 36, 56
Ping-Pong Team 42
PNK 25, 30
Pratt, Dirk 26, 32, 56
Pratt, Jane 56
Rao, Wesley 57
Raritan, Harold 57
Rasmussen, Stephen 57
Rastrussen, Timothy 46
Ratliff, Darren 57
Riggs, Daniel 36, 56
Rios, Javier 24, 57
Robinson, Kayleigh 57
Rocha, Ronald 57
Rollins, Tammy 15, 57
ROR 24, 30, 31
Rosales, Wanda 56

Sampson, Gregory 57
Sanderson, George 26, 32, 57
Scare Games 22, 23, 30-31, 32
School of Aviation 20
School of Business 18-19
School of Engineering 14-15
School of Liberal Arts
    and Monstrosities 16-17
School of Scaring 12-13
School of Science 20-21
school spirit 8
Scratchet, Emma 57
Scream Can Design 15
Shea, Trey 7, 57
Singh, Victor 58
Sitron, Vansantha 46
Skaren, Robert 35, 58
Skink, Lydia 58
Smile Squad 7
Snagglebottom, Darryl 59
Sobotka, Robert 55, 59
Soohoo, Donna 28, 59
Sosa, Albert 59
Squibbles, Scott "Squishy" 29, 58, 60
Steslicki, Violet 28, 58
Stillwater, Maggie 58
Sugiyama, Manami 59
Sullivan, James 29, 40, 59
Terrell, Ralph 59
Tsui, Weiqin 59
Turbeek, Filbert 47
Veigh, Ray 7, 58
Viscous State 39
von Limbergoop, Furgie 58
Walker, Pamela 58
Wazowski, Mike 7, 29, 32, 52, 59
Wei, Fay 7, 59, 60
Wheeler, Claire 23, 31, 58, 60
Williams, Carrie 25, 58
Wilsterbury, Cathy 47
Woodruff, Russell 42
Wooten, Paul 19, 58
Worthington, Johnny 24, 59
Xiao, Zane 42
Yearbook 36
Zaragoza, Adolfo 59

GOOD LUCK AT MONSTER INC

Written by Calliope Glass. Illustrated by Lorelay Bove and Scott Tilley.

Special thanks to Ricky Nierva, Kelsey Mann, Craig Foster, Winnie Ho, Brooke Dworkin,
Kiki Thorpe, Kelly Bonbright, LeighAnna MacFadden, and Margo Zimmerman.

Printed in the United States of America
First Edition
1 3 5 7 9 10 8 6 4 2
G942-9090-6-13091
Library of Congress Catalog Card Number: 2012953592

ISBN 978-1-4231-7009-9

For more Disney Press fun, visit www.disneybooks.com

SUSTAINABLE FORESTRY INITIATIVE
Certified Sourcing
www.sfiprogram.org
SFI-00993
For Text Only

Disney PRESS
New York

Little Green,
I think I'm finally getting outta this place thanks to your tuftoning sessions.

Big Red

Hi Mike!
It was super fun competing with you in the scare games this year! I totally had fun! I hope your summer is SUPER!

Carrie xoxo

P.S. next time, I'll totally tear you to pieces! ☺

Dude, let's get a hot sludge sundae sometime this summer. You rock! 
— Walter Mooney

You rock!

Great meeting you in Scream Can Design. Best Class Ever!
— Tammy Rollins

DUDE! AWESOME MEETING YOU THIS

MICHAEL,

MICHAEL- IT WAS A
PLEASURE HAVING YOU IN
MY CLASS. REMEMBER TO
PICK UP MY NEW BOOK, THE
FASCINATING HISTORY OF
SCREAM CANISTERS, AVAILABLE
IN THE FALL.

-PROFESSOR
BRANDYWINE

I can still run circles
around you, Wazowski!

Brynn Larson

See you at the Growl! Mark McDermott

Mike, you're like a big brother
to me. I mean, a smaller brother
who's also a big brother who's not my
real brother. You know what I mean?

-Terri